Gretel Killeen started writing comedy by accident when she stood up to perform a very serious poem and everybody laughed.

From here she moved to writing and performing comedy in a variety of theatres and clubs across Australia and for a number of radio stations including 2JJJ, 2MMM and 2 Day-FM. Gretel's comedy writing then led to television, where she appeared regularly on shows such as 'The Midday Show' with Ray Martin, 'The Big Gig', 'TVTV' and 'Coast to Coast'. She can currently be seen on Foxtel's 'Beauty and the Beast' and heard on 2BL and Regional ABC.

In the past seven years she has published a number of best selling books including *My Life is a Toilet, The* My Life is a Toilet *Instruction Book, The* My Life is a Toilet *Diary, My Sister's a Yoyo*, and *Cherry Pie*. She also writes for magazines and contributes her own humorous column to *The Australian* Magazine.

Gretel lives in Sydney's inner city with her two children.

my Sister's an Alien

**For
Zeke and Eppie and Mum and Dad.
GK**

**For Jenny McDermott.
LH**

Random House Australia Pty Ltd
20 Alfred Street, Milsons Point NSW 2061
http://www.randomhouse.com.au

Sydney New York Toronto
London Auckland Johannesburg
and agencies throughout the world

First published in 1998, reprinted 1999
Text copyright © Gretel Killeen 1998
Illustrations copyright © Leigh Hobbs 1998

National Library of Australia
Cataloguing-in-Publication Data

My sister's an alien.

ISBN 0 09 183902 5.

1. Australian wit and humour. I. Killeen, Gretel, II. Hobbs, Leigh.

A823.3

Cover, title and half title pages designed by Andrew Hoyne Design.
Text design and typesetting by Monkeyfish and Asset Typesetting Pty Ltd.
Author photograph (inside front cover) by Reece Scannell.
Illustrator photograph (inside back cover) by Francis Reiss.
Printed by Griffin Press Pty Ltd

My Sister's an Alien

Gretel Killeen
Leigh Hobbs

A Mark Macleod Book

RANDOM HOUSE

AUSTRALIA

To Haley
Love from
Grandma Liz
and Grandpa Bob
July 2000

It's not every day that your sister
shrinks to the size of a strawberry,
gets tangled in your yoyo and ends
up in outer space ... but that's what
had happened so far today.

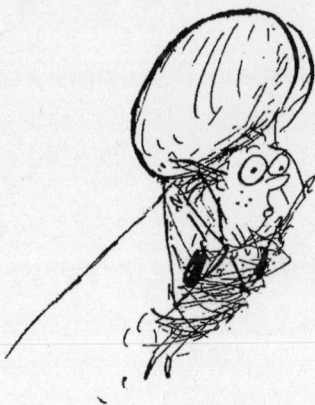

Early this morning Zeke got bored while he was sitting in the car waiting for his mum to take him to school, so he burped the alphabet, picked his nose, did a little fart, checked under the seats for jewelled boxes of hidden treasure and found his precious yoyo instead. Then he offered his sister two million dollars if she would get out of the car and play yoyos with him but while she was leaning out of the car she fell out the window, landed in a pothole, got run over by a truck that was carrying a house and got squished to the size of a strawberry. Now, Zeke knew that he had to stretch his sister back to her normal size but before he did that he thought he might whirl his yoyo on Eppie's head just for a bit of fun, but it got tangled up really badly in her hair and that's when their mum finally came out of the house to

drive Eppie and Zeke to school.
So Zeke hid Eppie in the bottom of
his schoolbag and then Eppie
ended up getting dropped down a
toilet, stuffed in a bin, stuck up a
tree, confiscated by the teacher,
stolen by a bird, pinched by a
puppy, stuck in a bike wheel,
grabbed by a garbage truck,
mistaken for a tennis ball, stolen
by a bully and saved by Zeke who,
at the very end of the day, was going
to untangle Eppie from the yoyo
and stretch her back to normal size
(just in time for Mum to pick them
both up from school and never be
any the wiser), but he unfortunately
decided to do some tricks with
Eppie attached to the yoyo first ...
Walk the Dog, Rock the Cradle,
Bite Your Bum and Around the
World. And it was while he was doing
this particular trick that the yoyo
string broke, and off Eppie went ...

all the way round the world.

So, Eppie was attached to Zeke's yoyo looping round the planet.

Meanwhile Mum had arrived to collect both her children from school, and Zeke was standing all alone in the playground desperately wondering if he should:

a) tell his mum that her daughter was lost in outer space and somehow, quite skilfully, make it all Eppie's fault

or b) invite all his friends over to help him celebrate the fact that his sister had flown off the face off the Earth and his wish had finally come true.

or c) run after Eppie and try to save her

or d) just stand there and act like nothing had happened.

Well, Zeke was feeling a little lazy and so he chose d) just stand there and act like nothing had happened. 'Dum de dum,' he sang to himself, 'Dum de dum hoola de dum.'

Mum was getting closer so Zeke tried to think of what he might say should his mum happen to ask 'Do you know where Eppie is?' 'Um, who?' he could say. 'I don't know anyone by that name. Perhaps you mean that poodle over there.' Or else he could say, 'She's gone to play at a friend's? Uh, she's on detention? A wizard put a spell on her and turned her into dog poop. Or actually she's been kidnapped, and the kidnappers want a huge ransom that I know we can't afford so I suggest it would be cheaper to buy another sister. '

(Actually, Zeke realised, that last excuse was not a very good one because there's no way anyone would believe that a kidnapper would want a ransom for Eppie. More likely after five minutes with Eppie, the kidnappers would pay Mum to take her back).

Mum was waving. She was getting

close. Act normal, thought Zeke, act normal.

She was coming closer and he was nearly acting normal except that he was bouncing up and down like a tennis ball and opening and closing his mouth so fast he looked like a mixture of a wide-mouthed frog and windscreen wipers stuck on FAST. (Please note that although boys do often act very weird this is not what Zeke normally looks like.)

'Oh my goodness,' thought Zeke. 'I should quit bouncing, shut my mouth and stop my eyes from blinking because otherwise Mum will definitely get suspicious and even though she won't know exactly what's happened she'll punish me anyway. It could be terrible, it could be horrible: much worse than having a sister!'

But actually Zeke need not have worried, because his mum didn't seem to notice anything odd at all and walked straight past him to the middle of the playground where she bent down and kissed a small tree.

'Yahooooooooooooooooo,' Zeke whispered softly. 'Mum's forgotten her glasses again.'

'Perfect,' thought Zeke. 'Mum's blind as a bat and there's no way I'm

telling her where her glasses are.'
(You see, much as Zeke adored his
mum, he rather enjoyed his life as
well, and although he apparently
talked far too much in class and only
tried half as hard as he could, Zeke
was smart enough to realise that if he
told his mum where her glasses were
she would immediately see that Eppie
was missing and he would of
course cop all the blame.) So Zeke
said nothing and ran off to the school
sports equipment room where he
borrowed a tennis racquet.

'Hi, Mum,' said Zeke when he
returned and gave his mum a peck on
the cheek.

'Hello, Darling. Have you seen
Eppie?'

'Yes, she's here,' said Zeke holding
up the tennis racquet. 'But she's lost
her voice so she can't say too much.'

'Oh dear,' said Mum. 'Eppie's voice
probably just needs a rest. Voices get

tired too you know.' And with that Mum kissed the tennis racquet on the head, said "there, there" and the three of them got into the car.

During the drive home Mum sang her favourite song, *Achy Breaky Heart*, which made all the dogs they passed on the way howl very loudly. Zeke was of course completely embarrassed, but when you're in the middle of pretending your sister is a tennis racquet you are really in no position at all to criticise others.

And so, instead of groaning and rolling his eyes as he normally would when his Mum sang *Achy Breaky Heart*, Zeke decided to pick a fight with the tennis racquet, just so Mum would think everything was normal.

'M-u-m, Eppie's pinching me,' said Zeke. 'Mu-u-um, she's kicking me. Mu-u-um, Eppie just poked her tongue out!'

'Quiet, you two,' said Mum as she drove with her head stuck right out the window because she thought it might help her see a little better. 'Quiet, you two or you'll have no TV for the rest of your lives.'

'Good,' said Zeke to himself. 'Mum doesn't suspect a thing.'

Once they got home, things were really pretty good for a while. Zeke of course got to eat twice as much afternoon tea and when Mum realised that Eppie hadn't eaten a crumb she sent the tennis racquet off to bed.

'I'll take her,' said Zeke, acting

really kind. 'You just keep looking for your glasses.'

'Oh that's so sweet of you,' said Mum. 'And when you get back down we'll have a nice piece of chocolate cake.'

('Actually,' Zeke thought, 'I'd rather have a new yoyo.')

All alone in Eppie's room, he tucked the tennis racquet into bed, looked around and quietly began to think seriously what the rest of his life would be like without his little sister ... 'Fantastic!' he decided.

That night Zeke got to watch whatever he wanted on TV, his mother did nearly all his homework, and he got to stay up extra late. But then, just when he was about to clean his teeth and go to bed, his Mum said, 'I'll be up in a minute to give you a hug. I'll just give Eppie her cuddle first.'

'No!' yelled Zeke, jumping up from the couch. 'You can't hug her ... because ... because ... because ... because for all we know she might have some disgusting disease where your ears blow up ... and your nose explodes ... and your legs and arms fall off. You can't hug her. If you do, you might die! And then I'd die of starvation and Gran and Pops would die of shock and then all the neighbours would come to look at our bodies and they'd catch the disease and they'd all die and all their friends and relatives too. So basically, Mum, if you go up and hug Eppie now you could end up killing at the very least forty seven thousand million people and their pets who need to be fed!'

'Zeke, sick little children need to hug their mothers, so I simply must hug Eppie. But if it will make you worry any less, I'll tie a hanky round my mouth and stick a peg on my nose. Now then, I'll look for my glasses for just one more minute and then I'll be up to hug you both.'

'Oh no,' thought Zeke. 'What should I do? My life is about to be completely over and I never even got to grow my hair really long and play the drums in a rock band. If Mum finds her glasses and sees that Eppie's a tennis racquet I am definitely going to be dead. Oh, please somebody save me!!!!!!!!!!!!'

Now sometimes, if you make enough wishes throughout your life and none of them ever comes true,

the wish accountants who wear suits
and live up in the clouds realise that
you're owed a really big wish, and
that's the wish they'll try to fulfil. Get
it? So that's what happened to Zeke.
He hadn't had any wishes come true
for ages and ages (except the wish
that his sister would disappear, but
that one didn't really count because
she was still haunting him anyway).
So the wish accountants decided it
was time for Zeke to be given a really,
really big wish and they made this
wish come true. (Of course this
meant that none of his other wishes
would ever come true: he would never
win the lottery or be given a Ferrari
or represent Australia playing football
... but Zeke decided he'd just happily
blame Eppie for all of this.)

So what do you think happened?
Do you think Zeke's strawberry-sized
sister suddenly dropped from the
skies and came plonking down the

chimney, where she got stuck just long enough in the grate for Zeke to pull her out by her feet and stretch her back to normal size, so their mother never discovered there'd been one single problem and they lived happily ever after and became incredibly rich and all became actors on *Neighbours*?

Brrrrrrrrrrrrrr, drum roll please!

No, nothing so fabulously exciting unfortunately. What happened exactly then and there was that the family cat walked past Zeke, and he was wearing Zeke's mother's glasses. Fantastic! Mum wouldn't find them for a million years.

The cat often secretly borrowed glasses because he liked to read, but his eyesight was getting worse. Of course he knew that he really should go to the eye doctor and get his own set of reading glasses, but the nearest animal eye doctor was a dog

and there was no way this cat was
going there.

'Thanks, wish accountants,' Zeke
said to the ceiling. 'Although I do
agree with the kids who are reading
this book and think you really could
have done a whole lot better and just
dropped Eppie down the chimney.'
Then Zeke grabbed the biggest fattest

book he could find (a cookbook on one thousand and one things to do with fish), showed it to the cat and put the book and the cat outside the back door. 'Enjoy your read,' he said to the cat. 'And take all the time you want.'

Then Zeke went back inside.

'This is great,' thought Zeke. 'Mum won't find her glasses for ages now.' And he sat down to relax, put his feet up on the coffee table, stick his finger in his ear and see if any mice were living in there. But suddenly he interrupted himself as he shrieked,

'**Oh no,**' and got such a shock he jabbed his finger so far into his ear that it almost popped out the other side. 'I forgot that in about twenty seconds Mum's going upstairs to kiss a tennis racquet good night!' said Zeke. 'I'd better find go and find an ugly doll that Mum can cuddle instead.'

But up in Eppie's bedroom there was no doll that looked at all like Eppie (who by the way is not ugly and does not look like half a worm, no matter what Zeke says). There were seven Barbie dolls and a stuffed monkey and although Zeke thought the stuffed monkey did look a bit like his sister it was way too small.

Stomp, bump, crash, ow! It was his mother coming up the stairs. And so in absolute desperation, Zeke opened Eppie's wardrobe door, rummaged

through her clothes, found a nightie,
put it on, stuck a ribbon in his hair,
jumped straight into his little sister's
bed and pretended to be asleep ...
just in the nick of time.

'How are you feeling, Eppie?' said
Mum to the bedside lamp. 'Still can't
talk? Well never mind. Let Mummy
give you a hug to make you a whole
lot better.' First Mum hugged the
bedside lamp, then the chest of
drawers, the little chair, the beanbag,
the desk and the footstool until finally

she'd gone all the way round the room, tripped on the carpet, fallen onto the bed, and given Zekeppie her hug.

'Eeeeeeeek! ' squeaked Zeke, trying to sound like a girl.

'In the morning, as a special treat, we'll do your hair in braids,' said Mum. 'And if you're too sick to go off to school you can play with some of my make-up. In fact,' she paused for extra excitement, 'would you like to put on a little lipstick now, just to make you feel pretty?'

'Help,' thought Zeke. 'I'd rather fall into a black hole and spend the rest of my life being cuddled by slaters than wear one crumb of make-up.'

'Here's a beautiful red lipstick,' said his mother. 'So you can sleep looking just like Snow White.'And she put the lipstick on Zeke, tucked him into bed, kissed him goodnight, said,

'Sleep tight, Eppie. I'll just walk down the hall now and say sweet dreams to Zeke.'

Zeke waited calmly until his mother left the room and then he went into a complete panic. He waved his arms and his legs like an upside down cockroach, covered his face with Eppie's pillow and screamed like Tarzan …

aaaaa**aaaa**aaaaaaaaaaaaaaaa aaaaaa**aaaaa**aaaa**aaa**aa.

And then when he'd finished he caught a look at the pillow that was covering his face, saw a red lipsticked mouth smudged on it and screamed once more, only more softly aaaaaaaaaaaaagh. Gross.

'What will I do?' agonised Zeke. 'I'll never get back into my room in time for Mum to kiss me good night!' He wriggled and squirmed in

desperate panic, fell off the bed and
rolled around, more and more and
more until suddenly he found himself
wrapped tight in the lambswool rug
that normally lay on Eppie's floor.
And that's when he caught another
glimpse of himself in Eppie's
bedroom mirror. 'I look almost
exactly like a sheep,' he thought.
'Especially to someone who isn't
wearing her glasses.' And with that

he got on all fours while still wrapped
in the rug and went charging down
the hall to his bedroom, bleating
'Baaaaaaa' as he passed his mum.

Once in his room Zeke unwrapped
himself, shoved the rug into his
cupboard and dived into his bed.

'Good heavens, darling,' his mother
said to his baseball mit as she

bumbled through the door, ' I really must be very tired, because I've started seeing things.'

And with that the cat came barging through the door wearing Mum's glasses and carrying Mum's biggest fattest cookbook (about one thousand and one things to do with fish). Well of course Mum fainted onto the bed and fell flat on top of Zeke.

'Oh,' mumbled Zeke. 'I should have remembered that stupid cat did a speed reading course.'

So there Zeke was, still wearing his sister's nightie and a pretty pink bow in his hair, pinned underneath his collapsed mother. She was still as still and not saying a word and Zeke was worried that she might really have injured herself ... until he heard her start to snore and mumble, 'Oh yes, Leonardo di Caprio! Come and rescue me!'

But what was Eppie doing all this
time? Had she stopped flying round
the world and landed in some
extraordinary place? Was she skiing
Swiss slopes, fishing in Finland,
surfing in Samoa, digging diamonds
in Dubai or swimming in the sea with
silly seals? Or was she still as small
as a strawberry, attached to Zeke's
yoyo and flying round the world,
getting giddier and giddier and
giddier and yelling, 'Pass me a

bucket! I think I'm going to be sick.'

Well, I'll tell you. She did fly round and round and round the world high up in the sky, but then after a while she started to drift down, closer and closer to earth. France was right there underneath her and she was just about to get spiked in the bottom

by the Eiffel Tower when she flapped her arms like a bird to raise herself higher and was caught by a giant gust of hot air that pushed her up safe above the poking point. And the gust of wind blew her on and on.

'I could fly all the way home like this', thought Eppie as she flap flap flapped away.

As she flew over America a group of farmers tried to shoot her, a flock of lazy finches perched on her shoulders as they migrated to Brazil, the Tahitians tried to catch her in a net and put her in the zoo, and in England they wanted to eat her. But strawberry-sized Eppie flapped on and on until finally she got so exhausted that she caught the nearest passing cloud, sat on it and had a little snooze.

The sun was warm and snug as it shone down on the cloud but as Eppie slept, more and more clouds

joined onto hers. Clouds joined to the
sides, below and above until the
whole sky was filled with clouds, the
sun was hidden and Eppie got cold.
And that's when she woke up.

'Hey, how come it's so dark?' Eppie
wondered. 'It couldn't be night time
yet.' A crack of thunder and a blaze of
lightning and a most frightening roar
of wind followed—rushing, howling,
bellowing louder. And before Eppie

could click her heels and say, "There's No Place Like Home", she was caught inside the most terrifying twister.

Round and around and around she spun higher, faster, all in a twirl. 'I'm going to die,' Eppie gasped. 'I'm going to be sucked up, twisted and spat out. I'll never be able to see Mum again. I'll never eat ice cream or see my school friends or play at the beach or have another birthday. Oh this is an absolute disaster—except for one amazing thing: Zeke is going to get blamed for it!'

And with that Eppie was squeezed up higher into the tornado and whirled like a banana in a blender (and let me say here that it was just as well that she had tied her shoelaces with a double bow because otherwise there is no way her shoes would have stayed on).

Now one of the good things about

being twisted and turned and spun
around if you are a girl who has been
squashed to the size of a strawberry
is that all of the tugging and pulling
and whirling around does tend to
stretch you back to normal size. So
that's what happened to Eppie. Then
there was a great big pop, like the

sound you make with your finger and your mouth but much, much louder.

pop

and Eppie was blurted right out of that twister and upupup into space where she floated around for quite a while and then landed

thump

on a place called Planet Sock.

Meanwhile Zeke was still lying on his bed wearing his sister's nightie, a pink bow in his hair and a smudge of his mother's bright red lipstick, and being squished under the heavy sleeping weight of his absolutely exhausted mother who you may remember had just begun to snore. The room shook with every rumbling snort, the curtains flapped, the bed springs groaned and a gust of humphy-galumphy Mum— snore—air would go right up Zeke's nose and nearly make his hair blow off.

This torture continued for quite some time until Zeke got completely and utterly fed up and yelled out 'Oh, bottom!' (because he wasn't allowed to say "bum"). 'This is terrible,' he said. 'With all this noise the police are definitely going to come here to see what all the fuss is and try to rescue our family, but they'll only find Mum and me and they'll guess Eppie's been killed by Mum's elephant snoring—maybe sucked up her nose and got stuck in her brain. And then they'll have to take Mum's head off and clean her brain with a vacuum cleaner to look for Eppie and they won't find her of course and all the police and doctors will be so upset that they'll stop concentrating and probably sew Mum's head back on round the wrong way, which will make it impossible for her to sit down and have dinner with us, let alone hug us good night. Oh bottom, bottom, bottom.'

'Stop snoring, Mum!' Zeke ordered urgently. But it was too late, because just then there was a tap tap tap on the window and he looked up in fright. But it wasn't the police; it was, to Zeke's surprise, the three possums who lived in the attic. They were dressed in their party gear, bright

frocks and floral shirts, and were
very very mad.

'What on earth do you think you're
doing down here?' asked the biggest
possum whose name was Ralph
Gorgeous. 'We're trying to have a
party upstairs and no one can even
hear the band because of this terrible,
deafening, rumbling noise. It's
making the whole house shake and

shake and making our fabulous party drinks spill all over our lovely fur coats.'

'I'm sorry,' said Zeke. 'The noise is my mother. She's really tired from looking for her glasses, which are actually being worn by the cat. But I couldn't tell her that because if Mum had her glasses, then she would have seen that my stinker sister is nowhere to be found. So Mum would have asked me, "Zeke, where on earth is Eppie?" And I would have had to say, "Well actually, Mum, she's not on Earth at all; she's attached to my yoyo and is flying round the world ... oh and by the way she's shrunk to the size of a strawberry."'

'And then of course Mum would have got absolutely furious and confiscated the rest of my life ... and that's probably exactly what she will do when she wakes up ... straight after she's killed me!'

Then Zeke burst into tears (but he pretended that he just had a cold), gave a great big blow on his nose and then wiped the snot all over his sleeve.

'Ar yuk!' said the second possum whose name was Fluffybigbum. 'Don't be such an animal!'

'Do you think you could help me?' Zeke asked the three possums as they sat perched on the window dressed in

their party clothes which didn't
really fit because they'd been pinched
from neighbours' clotheslines.
'Could you spread the word on the
bush telegraph, perhaps ask the
flying fish, or the secretive snakes
or those gossipping goannas …
just spread the word that we need
to find where Eppie is because,
much to my regret, we have to get
her back.'

'Don't be ridiculous,' said the third
possum, whose name was
Nosewhistle Jo. 'Asking animals one
by one—I've never heard of anything
so primitive.'

'You're right of course,' Zeke
replied. 'I should hire a plane that
writes in the sky,

lost:
one stupid strawberry-sized sister,
contact Zeke,
and don't tell my Mum.

'Are you joking?' said Ralph Gorgeous. 'Or has some horrible slug slid in your ear and into your head and eaten half your brain? Because if you really want to find where Eppie is quick smart, I suggest you hop on the Internet.'

'But I don't know how to use the Internet,' moaned Zeke.

'Then we'll find Wise Old Owl and he can teach you,' said Nosewhistle Jo as he whistled *Hey diddly* through his nose.

'Well could you help get me out from under here first?' said Zeke in a muffled voice as his mother made one more enormous snore, rolled smack bang on top of him and said, 'I love you too, Tom Cruise.'

'Quick! Get me out of here!' said Zeke, and with that Fluffybigbum jumped off the window sill and into the bedroom, walked straight up to Mum and said in a very deep voice,

'Hello, I'm Tom Cruise. Follow me.'
And up Mum got and followed
Fluffybigbum the possum all the way
down the hall and safely to Mum's
room, where she fell fast asleep once
more, snoring like a dillion pigs.

Then, before you could make
whatever sound it is that a wise
old bird could make, bwa bwa,
bwa perhaps, The Wise Old Owl

flew in through the window with a flurry of feathers and smashed straight into the mirror. 'Ow!' said Owl. 'Those mirrors are horrid. Every time I look in one I think I've seen the most beautiful bird and break my beak trying to kiss it.'

'Are you sure this is The *Wise* Old Owl?' whispered Zeke to Nosewhistle Jo.

But it *was* The Wise Old Owl and pretty soon he was setting up the computer to send Zeke's message and find out just who in the world knew where Eppie was. 'This plug here, that button there, put this thingummyjig in that what-not,' said The Wise Old Owl as he ordered everybody in the room to assist with his important task. 'Okay,' he said finally. 'Now we're ready to type the message.'

'Message typed,' replied Zeke with pride.

'And now we shall send it off round the world,' bellowed The Wise Old Owl triumphantly. 'Watch me press this little red power switch.' And the whole thing went

Kaboom.

In fact the message wasn't sent to
computers all round the world, but
printed instead on each of The Wise
Old Owl's feathers, which had blown
right off in the explosion and were
now fluttering high into the sky to be

spread by the world's wandering winds.
'Oh no, I'm naked!' said The Wise

Old Owl. 'But at least the message has
been sent. Could someone hand me a
dressing gown while we wait for our
replies?'

Well Ralph Gorgeous lent Owl his
leopard skin coat and then they waited.

Wait, wait, wait, wait.

'Want a chocolate biscuit?' Zeke asked The Wise Old Owl.

'No thanks. I'm on a diet,' he replied.

Wait, wait, wait, wait.

And then with a hum and a whirr and a whiz, messages started flying in from every single corner of the globe … and some even came with photos. Yes, photos of what looked like a strawberry with something attached to its head. 'I wonder how they took those photos of Eppie?' thought Zeke.' Cameras always break when I try to photograph her.'

Someone even sent in a video in which you could very clearly see that Eppie was singing that song that made Zeke want to vomit every time he heard it, *I'm a Barbie Girl in a Barbie World!*

She'd been seen over Botswana, Croatia, Canada, Tasmania and Scandinavia. Some cow even sent a

message to say she'd seen Eppie
jumping over the moon.

But the most recent sighting had
been by two astrologers who were
visiting their mummies in Egypt.

They said they'd seen a girl dancing
way out on Planet Sock who was
singing a little song to herself called
My Brother Zeke is a Boy's Bra.

'That's her. That's her!' yelled happy
Zeke. 'That's my horrible, disgusting,
worm head, pig's bottom, bosom brain
sister. Yahoo! Let's go get her!'

'Not us,' said Ralph Gorgeous.
'We've got a party to go to and,
besides, we've done all we can.'

'Well if there's anything I can ever
do for you,' said Zeke, 'just plop down
through that man-hole in the ceiling.'

'Possum-hole,' corrected
Nosewhistle Jo.

'Actually, Zeke,' said Fluffybigbum,
'could I borrow that pretty dress
you're wearing?'

Zeke had forgotten he was wearing Eppie's nightie and was so embarrassed he shrieked, 'Aeiou!', ran from the room and tumble, tumble, tumbled down the stairs like a tennis ball.

And that's where he lay like a spilt laundry basket and dreamt that he blew up a thousand balloons, tied all of their strings to his belt and floated up, right up into space where he found his sister Eppie and made her promise that she would pay him a fee of a thousand dollars a week for the rest of their lives for the privilege of being his sister.

But then Zeke woke up and unfortunately remembered all the trouble that he was in.

'Oh no, oh no, a few hours to go before Mum wakes up and Eppie and my yoyo are still lost in space. How am I ever going to get up there?' he wondered as he lay on the floor rattling away, listening to his mother snore. 'You can't get a bus to space, or catch a train, or a plane, or walk, or run, or roll or skateboard or ... Hey, wait, I know! I could go to a circus, dress up as a clown and get them to blow me out of the cannon ... off the face of earth and into the starry skies ... or if that didn't work and worse came to worst I could fall in a pothole, get run over by a truck that is towing a house, get shrunk to the size of a strawberry, attached to a yoyo and hurled into the sky like a rocket ... Hey wait a minute!' said Zeke to himself. 'That's it—a rocket!'

Well of course Zeke tried to make his own space rocket using old toilet paper rolls, egg cartons and silver foil but the glue wouldn't dry and there was no sister to sit on things to make them stick better (because she was selfishly dancing on Planet Sock) and no mum to help with the cutting out (because she was upstairs, begging Tom Cruise to marry her, in between snoring like a fart cushion) and so in the end he snuck out the door, got on his bike and rode to the nearest space centre.

'Hello,' Zeke said, when the space centre's door was opened by a huge toothless purple-haired woman. 'Excuse me for bothering you so late in the night but I'd like to go on your next trip into space.'

'Oh that's nice,' said the toothless purple-haired woman. 'But I'm very sorry you can't come because what we need is males who are strong,

brave and fearless; we have enough
little girls with bows in their hair.'

'**What!**' gasped Zeke. Oh yes, the
nightie, and off he rode home to
quickly change into his Superboy suit

and once again knock on the space centre door.

'I'm very sorry, Superboy,' said the toothless purple-haired woman, 'but I'm afraid you're far too young. '

And with that Zeke said thank you and rode off into the night. Only to return ten minutes later wearing a false beard and a moustache.

'I'm very sorry, Mister Super,' said the toothless purple-haired woman, 'you're absolutely perfect except for one simple thing: you are far too thin.'

And off rode Zeke as fast as he could to find cotton wool to stick in his cheeks, and pillows to stuff down his suit so that every single part of his body seemed quite enormous and he looked like a balloon filled with marbles ... and he could hardly move.

S l o w l y Zeke got back onto his bike and s l o w l y he reached for the pedals and ever so s l o w l y he began to ride, back to the space centre.

'I'm terribly sorry,' said the toothless purple-haired woman. 'I'm sure you'd make the perfect astronaut, but you're just a moment too late. If you'd been here even a minute ago things might have been quite different but, as it happens, today's space probe is now full and leaving any second.'

'Bup!' said Zeke with his cheeks full of cotton wool. ' Bup, bup, bup, bup!' But the toothless purple-haired woman had already left, to eat mashed peanut butter and melted ice cream (mixed with a pinch of salt and scrambled snails) while she watched the latest space rocket take-off.

So Zeke stumbled along in his fat Superboy suit, beard and moustache, desperately looking for a way to get past the locked wire fences and onto the launch pad.

'Who's there?' said a voice from out on the tarmac.

'Pleath blet me in plast thith gade,' repeated Zeke.

'Listen, old fellow,' said the voice. 'Swallow whatever you've got in your mouth, then come here and tell me what you said.'

And so Zeke removed all the pillows and stuffing and his beard and moustache. Then he slipped under the big wire fence to walk towards the voice. And when he got right up to the voice, he found himself talking to the space rocket flight attendant who was dressed in a very nice, casual outfit with matching tie and little peaked cap. The attendant was just about to fasten all doors and check that all seatbelts were fastened when

Zeke said, 'Wait! I need a lift into space.'

'Sorry, Superboy,' said the attendant. 'We just gave the last seat to a shooting star who's a little bit sick with the flu. So you'll have to catch the next probe which leaves in about ... oh,' and with that the attendant looked at his watch. 'In about eleven years. Now get off the launching pad if you don't mind and go and stand somewhere safe.'

10 9 8 7

Are you thinking poor Zeke, he's missed his chance?

6 5 4

Well, not on your life!

3 2 1

Because what do you see if you look very closely?

ZEROBLASTOFF!

Look, right there on the pointy bit. Do you see a little person dressed as Superboy sort of making a face like he's sitting on something sharp? Well, guess who that is? It's Zeke, blasting through space with his mouth so wide open that he's just swallowed three flies and a pigeon.

Up, up, up he went, through the clouds, through the blue skies and beyond. Up to the rainbow, through the red, orange, yellow, green, blue,

indigo, violet, and up into space, dark
space where a zillion stars were
twinkling brightly saying, 'Zekie,
come and play with me.'

After seven hours, or maybe five
minutes, Zeke's bottom really began
to hurt. So he tried to get more
comfortable by doing a shift and a

wiggle but he slipped completely off the tip and began to slide down the space probe. 'Uh Oh,' said Zeke.

He tried to wrap his arms around the space probe, but he just kept slip sliding down. Down he slipped, down, down, and his eyes wide open with fear. He tried to grab hold of a wing as he slid, he tried to grab on with his legs. But down he slid with the engine flames getting closer. He was hot and scared and his hands were all slippery and he was gaining speed ... when all of a sudden he came to a halt as his Superboy suit got caught on the corner of the window and Zeke took a peek inside.

'Hello!' he called to the silver-suited astronauts as he tap tapped on the glass. 'Hello!' he bellowed. 'Could you help me, please?' But nobody heard him because they were all eating spacecorn, which is like popcorn only a gillion times louder. That's right

nobody paid him any attention at all
until all of a sudden the space probe
took a sharp turn to the left and Zeke
was hurled at the window and his
face squished up hard on the glass.
The astronauts heard a tremendous
thump, looked up to see Zeke's flat
face, and then all fainted into their
spacecorn buckets.

'Oh fabulous,' said Zeke, dangling from the window. 'Help me, you great fat burp heads!' And then he quietly began to cry, feeling very sorry for himself until he was rudely interrupted by a gentle rrrrrrrrrrripping sound. 'My pants!' shrieked Zeke. 'My Superboy suit is tearing!' And sure enough it was.

'This is all Eppie's fault,' mumbled Zeke bitterly as finally his suit tore completely off and once again he was caught in his undies. (Yep! The Barbie ones his mum gave him for Christmas last year, nineteen pairs for the price of one.) 'Help!' he screamed into the dark universe, as he was hurtled through the atmosphere.

'Help, help,' he called as he raced through the galaxy at a billion trillion zillion dillion hillion kilometres an hour. Heeeeeeeeeeeeeeeeeeeeeeeeeee eeeeeeeeeeeeeeeeeeeeeeeeeeeeeeeeee

eeeeeeeeeeeeeeeeeeeeeeeeeeeeeeeeeeeeeeee
eeeeeeeeeeeeeeeeeeeeeeeeeeeeeeeeeeeeeeee
eeeeeeeeeeeeeeeeeeeeeeeeeeeeeeeeeeeeeeee
eeeeeeeeeeeeeeeeeeeeeeeeeeeeeeeeeeeeeeee
eeeeeeeeeeeeeeeeeeeeeeeeeeeeeeeeeeeeeeee
eeeeeeeeeeeeeeeeeeeeeeeeeeeeeeeeeeeeeeee
eeeeeeeeeeeeeeeeeeeeeeeeeeeeeeeeeeeeeeee
eeeeeeeeeeeeeeeeeeeeeeeeeeeeeeeeeeeeeeee
eeeeeeeeeeeeeeeeeeeeeeeeeeeeeeeeeeeeeeee
eeeeeeeeeeeeeeeeeeeeeeeeeeeeeeeeeeeeeeee

eeeeeeeeeeeeeeeeeeeeeeeeeeeeeeeeeeeeee
eeeeeeeeeeeeeeeeeeeeeeeeeeeeeeeeeeeeee
eeeeeeeeeeeeeeeeeeeeeeeeeeeeeeeeeeeeee
eeeeeeeeeeeeeeeeeeeeeeeeeeeeeeeeeeeeee
eeeeeeeeeeeeeeeeeeeeeeeeeeeeeeeeeeeeee
eeeeeeeeeeeeeeeeeeeeeeeeeeeeeeeeeeeeee
eeeeeeeeeeeeeeeeeeeeeeeeeeeeeeeeeeeeee
eeeeeeeeeeeeeeeeeeeeeeeeeeeeeeeeeeeeee
eeeeeeeeeeeeeeeeeeeeeeeeeeeeeeeeeeeeee
eeeeeeeeeeeeeeeeeeeeeeeeeeeeeeeeeeeeee
eeeeeeeeeeeeeeeeeeeeeeeeeeeeeeeeeeeeee
eeeeeeeeeeeeeeeeeeeeeeeeeeeeeeeeeeeeee
eeeeeeeeeeeeeeeeeeeeeeeeeeeeeeeeeeeeee
eeeeeeeeeeeeeeeeeeeeeeeeeeeeeeeeeeeeee
eeeeeeeeeeeeeeeeeeeeeeeeeeeeeeeeeeeeee
eeeeeeeeeeeeeeeeeeeeeeeeeeeeeeeeeeeeee
eeeeeeeeeeeeeeeeeeeeeeeeeeeeeeeeeeeeee
eeeeeeeeeeeeeeeeeelp!

'Don't cry my little fellow,' said the kind deep voice of The Man in the Moon as he caught Zeke in his great big hand. 'Here put this cheese suit on and cover up those Barbie Doll undies.'

'I can't wear a suit made out of cheese,' replied Zeke.

'Oh, all right then,' said The Man in the Moon. 'If you want everyone to see your ...'

'Okay, okay, 'interrupted Zeke as he grabbed the suit made of cheese and The Man in the Moon.

While The Man in the Moon whispered in his ear, 'My mum gave me twelve pairs of Barbie Doll undies for my birthday, and boy do I know they're embarrassing.'

Once he was dressed in the cheese suit, which I must say wasn't all that warm because it was full of holes, Zeke told The Man in the Moon all about strawberry-sized Eppie, the possums, the owl, the Internet, the kaboom, the astronomers, and even his mother's loud snoring.

'So that's what that dreadful noise is,' said The Man in the Moon.

And sure enough, when Zeke

stopped sobbing, even though he was
sitting on the moon, he could still
hear his mother's dreadful snorts.

'So you see, my sister Eppie was
last seen up in space and I absolutely

have to find her before my mum
wakes up and blames me and yells
and screams and carries on until my
ears burst and my head explodes and
I'm stuffed and put in a museum. And
besides,' continued Zeke very softly, 'I
want my yoyo back.'

'Oh I understand,' said The Man in
the Moon, or Moonie as he liked to be
called. 'I used to have a yoyo myself
but I dropped it one day and it fell to
Earth ... and created the Grand
Canyon I believe. But enough of that.
Tell me, son, where was little Eppie
last seen?'

'Well some astronomers saw her on
Planet Sock. Do you know where that
is?'

'Haven't got a clue,' said Moonie.
'But I've got a Planet Directory. Let's
hop on my new space motorbike, take
it for a spin and find this sister of
yours.' And that's exactly what they
set off to do.

They jumped onto Moonie's lovely cheese space motorbike and went racing off the surface of the moon, far away and into space, stopping off at the Milky Way to get a couple of milkshakes.

'Yeehaa!' they both squealed and they giggled so hard that they nearly fell off twice.

'Hold on tight,' said The Man in The Moon. 'And keep your eye out for dangerous unidentified flying objects.'

'You mean aliens?' asked Zeke.

'No. I mean humans in silver suits eating spacecorn and fainting while they career around the neighbourhood in space rockets,' said Moonie.

And so they sped through space, ducking and weaving around all the stars, in a sky space called Hollywood, then through bright light and into black holes, all the while laughing and giggling and fighting over who was taking up too much of the seat. And then with a sudden screech of brakes Moonie said, 'First stop, Pluto for petrol. '

On Pluto, they checked the Planet

Directory but couldn't find Planet
Sock anywhere, so they asked the
petrol attendant who was a dribbling
big-eared pup.

'Dar,' he said in a deep slow voice. '
Um ah I don't know. Try the next
stop. Those Martians know lots of
things.'

And so Moonie and Zeke rode to
Mars, which is a planet made of
chocolate with a caramel centre, and
they asked two flubbery Martians if

they knew where Planet Sock was,
but their ears were so covered with
folds of fat that they couldn't even
hear the question.

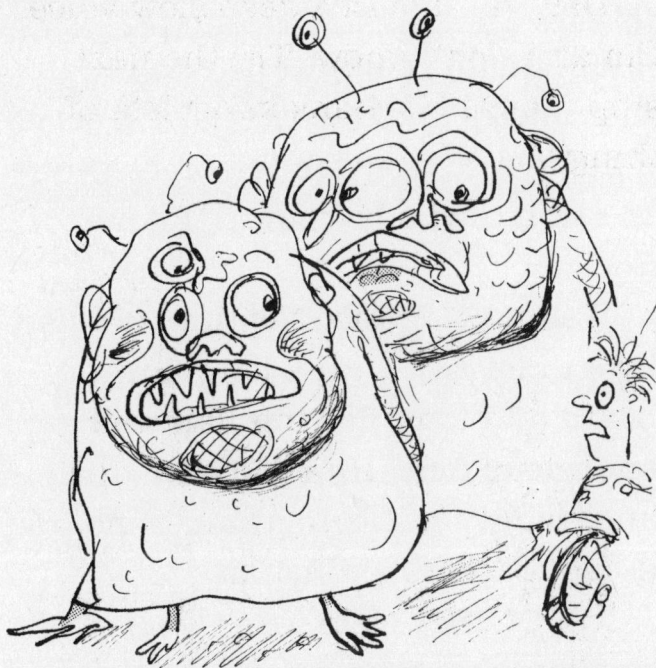

Next stop was Venus, the planet of
love, and Zeke and Moonie hadn't
even turned off the engine before a
hundred long-haired girls ran up and
tried to cuddle them. 'Oh puke,' said
Zeke and The Man in the Moon. 'Let's

get out of here! Girls' germs, girls' germs,' they both screamed together and off they went scared to billyo that they might be hugged and kissed to death.

So, finally, completely covered in kiss marks and desperate for a scrub-a-dub wash, they landed on Neptune to ask if anybody knew of Planet Sock.

Well now, Planet Neptune is ruled by a giant fish with a long flowing beard and long flowing hair and an enormous fork. He's bad and mean and mighty unclean, afraid of no one except barbers and baths.

'Oh pong!' said Zeke. 'This guy smells worse than Eppie.' And on they went to ask their question.

'Excuse me, Sir,' said The Man in the Moon pinching his nose tightly. 'You don't habben to doe where a place called Pladed Sog bight be?'

'Of course I do, but I'm not telling

you,' roared the King. 'Now get out of
here!'

'Bud please, Sir, 'continued brave
Zeke while he also pinched his nose
tight. 'I deed to doe where Pladed
Sog is so I cad fide by sisda.'

'Sister?' bellowed the King. 'She
wouldn't happen to be beautiful
would she?'

'Dot in de least,' said Zeke disgustedly. 'Eppie looks like a plasdicine chihuahua.'

'Well I've heard on the satellite that a beautiful girl landed on Planet Sock. She arrived wearing some sort of round crown on her head and the people there made her their Queen.'

'Oh, my gosh!' gasped Zeke in a whisper. 'That round crown is my precious yoyo and so the girl wearing it must be Eppie. But how could anyone think that she was beautiful, when she looks like an ugly chihuahua?'

'I heard that,' boomed the mighty mean Neptune. 'And how dare you speak badly of my son's future wife!'

'Wod?' said Zeke. 'You bust be jokig.'

'Do I look like I have a sense of humour?' grumped King Neptune.

'Doe,' said Zeke quietly, 'bud you loog lige you should ged wud.'

'Get out of my sight!' thundered Neptune.

'Doe, waid!' said Moonie, 'We deed to find de girl.'

'Well I'm damned if I'm going to tell you where she is,' laughed the king, 'because we're off to get her for ourselves.'

And with that Neptune and his son Nipper slid onto their beautiful flying white horses and charged off to Planet Sock.

'Follow those horses,' Zeke yelled to Moonie who was so impressed by the Neptunes' horsepower he was thinking he should possibly get a faster space motorbike.

'Follow them, please!' screeched Zeke one more time.

'Pardon,' said Moonie in a daze.

'Oh forget it,' said Zeke as he grabbed for the space motorbike. 'Just hop onto the back.'

Well now, I don't know if you've

ridden a space motorbike made of cheese, but it's not that easy to do. Especially if you've got a huge Man in the Moon plopped heavily on the back. Vrooooooooooooom went the engine, then they both tumbled off.

Then they clambered back on and the engine vroomed again and they kangaroo-hopped along the surface of Planet Neptune until they tipped over once again.

'Oh for heaven's sake, let me do it,' said Moonie.

'No,' said Zeke. 'It's my turn.'

'But it's my bike.'

'Well it's my turn.'

'My bike.'

'My turn.'

And so they continued arguing like seagulls until the flapping wings of the flying horses could no longer be heard.

Then Zeke said, 'Hey what's that over there?' and while Moonie turned to look at absolutely nothing, Zeke hopped on the bike and headed off into space with Moonie hanging on the back. But unfortunately, not for long.

'Weeeooo, weeooo' came the sound of the Planet Police sirens. 'Weeeooo,weeeeooooo. Pull over or we'll be forced to shoot!'

So Zeke of course did pull over with a bump and a screech, and the Planet Police pulled up right beside him on their brand new glowing gold spaceboards.

'You're both under arrest for driving dangerously and must come with us to the Police station,' said the two little crimson police dressed in their cool sky surfing gear.

Zeke and Moonie wanted to escape but didn't have a sultana-sized idea how. So they hopped on the back of the spaceboards and caught the waves and currents of the heavens toward the station. That is until they

were suddenly ambushed by a space-
ship full of screaming girls from
Venus.

'Hi, boys. We've come to rescue
you!' squealed the girlie girls. And
that's exactly what they did. They
swooped by on their pretty pink
skycycles, plonked the boys on the
handlebars, and then pedalled far
away.

It was great, they had escaped, but there was still a problem because the girls had no desire to chase Neptune and Nipper all the way to Planet Sock. That's right: the girls wanted to go dancing with Zeke and Moonie, then play hide and seek and spin the bottle.

'There is no way I'm doing any of that,' said Zeke. ' I would rather live in a toilet.'

'Me too,' replied The Man in the Moon. 'We've got to jump off here before we're violently ill.'

'Not on your life,' laughed the girls' leader, a tall strong girl with bright red hair called Vanessa Venus. 'There's no way you're running away from us, and I'm going to make sure of it!' And with that she threw a handful of pink-magic-kissing dust at Zeke and Moonie and then began to laugh loudly. 'This will make you want to hug and kiss us every minute of every day for the rest of your lives.'

Well it worked on Moonie who was so completely covered by the magic dust that it even went into his ears, nose, eyes and mouth. But it didn't work at all on Zeke because he is allergic to dust and he just sneezed it all off.

'Quick!' yelled Zeke. 'Off we go.'

'No, I'm very happy here,' said Moonie as he kissed and cuddled the gaggle of girls.

So Zeke jumped from the skycycle handlebars with a "yahoo" and luckily landed on the roof of a passing space taxi, which was a free service provided by the local council and looked a bit like a chocolate doughnut but moved a whole lot faster.

'To Planet Sock please,' Zeke said to the driver who was a small slimy yellow fellow with three heads.

'Of course, of course, of course,' the driver replied, and so off they went.

Pretty soon they caught up with Neptune and Nipper and were close enough to even overhear their secret conversation, which was about Prince Nipper not keeping his bedroom tidy enough, and therefore not being allowed to watch any TV until he'd picked everything up.

Suddenly the Neptunes spotted Zeke and drew their special silver arrows to fire at him as he passed. But the cab driver drove like a football star, ducking and weaving and spinning and turning and never once receiving even a scratch on his bumper bar. The Neptunes were furious. Who was this smarty pants? And they ordered their horses to fly faster.

Leaping over planets and galloping across galaxies, they raced at a pace through space until Zeke arrived on Planet Sock a good ten minutes before the Neptunes.

'Thank you,' Zeke said to the cab driver as he waved him goodbye.

Thinking he was all alone, Zeke started to wander about Planet Sock and soon realised the entire planet was made out of nothing but socks. The ground was socks, the trees were socks, the cars, the houses, the pets and the people were all socks.

'Aha,' thought Zeke. ' I get it now! Planet Sock's the place where all those socks go when they disappear from the washing.' (Suddenly he remembered home, and the hurry he was in to rescue his sister and get his yoyo back before his snoring Mum woke up.)

'Hello,' said a red sock.

'Hello,' said Zeke. 'I'm wondering if you can help me. Have you seen a silly girl called Eppie who has a yoyo stuck in her hair?'

'What did you say?' said the red sock. 'A silly girl called Eppie?

Officers! Arrest this boy!'

'Why?' squeaked Zeke. 'What have I done?'

'You've spoken badly of our queen, you traitor!'

'What?' said Zeke. 'Stupid Eppie is your queen?'

'Double arrest this man,' said the red sock. And with that a whole army of socks (about a drawer full) arrested Zeke (but only once, because they didn't have a clue how to double arrest anything).

Anyway, the socks took Zeke off to jail, and may I say the socks all marched very well, and when they got to the jail it was also made of socks, boys' sports socks, and they

stank!

But that's where Zeke sat, in the pongo sock jail for what seemed like days and days and days, but was probably about fifteen minutes. Then there was a fanfare of trumpets (which actually sounded a little muffled because socks are not great trumpet players) and Zeke was escorted to the magnificent Sock Garden, that quite honestly just looked like a pile of washing.

'All rise to meet Her Majesty,' said the leader of the army, a rather attractive tall blue sock with a gold circle round the top. And with that Queen Eppie arrived.

'Hello, stranger in a cheese suit. My name is Queen Eppie. Welcome to my Queendom.'

'Eppie, it's me,' whispered Zeke.

'Me who?' replied Queen Eppie.

'Me, Zeke your brother, you stupid git!'

'Aaaaaagh don't you call me a stupid git,' said Eppie, 'or I won't tell you that I've been lying here really

missing home while I listened to
Mum and her snoring.'

'Missing home!' said Zeke, not
believing. 'What is there to miss?
Here you're a queen and spoilt rotten.'

'Well actually, Zeke, I'm pretty
bored. Whenever I want to get up and
do anything some sock goes and does
it for me.'

'Gosh Eppie,' scolded Zeke. 'Have you been hit on the head? You used to be the laziest fuzzhead that I've ever met, and I was quite proud of you. Anyone else would dream of this life. I can only imagine that you're very ill and I must get you home immediately, because other than that you're an ungrateful dingbat.'

'Am not.'

'Are so.'

'Am not.'

'Are too.'

'Guards!' called Eppie. 'Take this silly boy away and hang him from the clothesline.'

And hundreds of socks came towards Zeke, making frightening faces as they marched. But they actually looked cute instead of scary and Zeke wanted to reach down and cuddle them. Luckily, however, he came to his senses and, as the sock guards reached out for Zeke, he grabbed the whole bunch and tied them up in a knot.

'Now come with me,' Zeke ordered his sister.

'No, I've changed my mind,' said Eppie. 'You're absolutely right about this place being good. So I've decided that this is where I should stay.'

'Well, that's bad luck cause I'm taking you home.'

'But ...,' said Eppie.

'There's no time for buts,' said Zeke urgently as he heard the distant thunder of hooves. 'I have to take you right here and now because King Neptune is somewhere here on this planet, ready to kidnap you and make you marry his son!'

'Oh fantastic!' said Eppie. 'Then I'm definitely staying. I hear Prince Nipper is gorgeous.'

'You come with me, Eppie,' ordered Zeke. 'Or else I'm dobbing to Mum.'

The flying horses were coming closer.

Zeke jumped for cover up a green sock tree and the socks shrieked, screamed and squelched (which is a sort of high piercing noise that socks make when they're afraid).

But Eppie stood very straight right in the middle of the garden, smoothing her hair, neatening her gown, fluttering her eyelids like a film star and trying to make her bosoms look enormous, even though she actually didn't have any.

'I hope he's rich,' wished Eppie. 'With a boat and a palace and a sister I can play with. And I hope I shall have beautiful clothes and jewels and parties and cakes and lollies. And I hope that he is as handsome as a dream.'

The flurry of horses came closer and halted right before Eppie. She waited for the sock dust and lint to settle, then slowly opened her eyes while puckering her lips as though ready for a most romantic kiss ... and lo and behold if she didn't get a kiss, a great big wet sloppy kiss that smelt a lot like fish.

'Oh gross!' screamed Eppie as she opened her eyes and saw that Prince Nipper was a fishhead.

'Aaaaaaaaaaaaaaaaaaaaaaaaa aaaaaaaaaaaaaaaaaaaaaaaaaaaa aaaaaaaaaaaaaaaaaaaaaaaaaaaa aaaaaaaaaaaaaaaaaaaaaaaaaaaa aaaaaaaaaagh!' shrieked Eppie.

'Follow me,' yelled Zeke.

But Nipper had grabbed Queen Eppie with his slimy fish fins and was laughing delightedly.

'Help,' Eppie blurted out.' Help me, Zeke. I promise I'll eat all your yucky vegetables for absolutely ever.' Suddenly Eppie thought she needn't have bothered to make such a big promise because Nipper was so slippery he was losing his grip on her anyway, and down she slid, swish boom bah, and landed softly on the sock ground underneath. But she still needed rescuing.

'Do you promise you'll eat my yucky vegetables?' demanded Zeke.

'Yes,' said Eppie sulkily.

'Pinky then,' said Zeke holding out his little finger.

'Pinky,' said Zeke touching Zeke's little finger with hers. And so the deal was done. Eppie would eat Zeke's yucky vegetables and Zeke would rescue her. Then before you could say 'sock a doodle do' the brother and sister were holding hands and running away as fast as they could.

'After them!' yelled King Neptune. And off they went through the sock town, chasing Queen Eppie and Zeke, over the sock bridge, past the sock tower, through the sock shops, the sock schools and the sock hospital that was busy repairing all the sick socks with holes in their heels and their toes.

'Dive,' yelled Zeke.

'Dive where?' yelled Eppie.

'This is no time for questions,' scolded Zeke as he picked Eppie up by the scruff of the neck and threw her into a huge football sock that was on his way home from a game, and then threw himself in straight after.

'Sssssshh,' said Queen Eppie to the football sock. 'Don't tell a sole we're in here.' ("Sole", get it?)

'Of course, Your Majesty. You smell like fish, I assume you're escaping from Prince Nipper? Leave it up to me.'

And they were all perfectly quiet as the football sock walked to the airport with his precious cargo, and no one would ever have known what he was hiding inside if it weren't for one very simple thing—Zeke's yoyo was still attached to Eppie's head and poking out the top.

'There they are!' yelled King Neptune. And so the football sock ran as fast as he could while his

passengers cried, 'Help us!'

But no one paid any attention because they couldn't quite understand what Zeke and Eppie had said.

'*Melt us*? What does that mean?' said the sock crowd that had gathered.

'No,' yelled Queen Eppie. 'Help us.'

'Oh, eat puss!' said the crowd. ' Well that really is disgusting.'

'No, you ninnies!' roared Queen

Eppie. 'For heaven's sake, catch those suckers behind us.'

And the sock people replied, 'Oh, okay.' But the socks had absolutely no luck at all. They tried lying on the road and tripping the baddies. They even tried jumping from the trees and strangling the Neptunes. But absolutely nothing seemed to work and the Neptunes were only a few horse lengths away as Zeke and Eppie and the football sock entered Planet Sock Airport.

'When is the next flight to Earth?' said the football sock to the frilly sock airport receptionist.

'Oh we haven't any direct flights to Earth,' she said. ' We only have a falling star that is going to Mercury, and a comet that is going to Jupiter.'

'Have you nothing at all that is going to Earth?' begged Queen Eppie from inside the footy sock.

'Is that you, Queen Eppie?' said the

receptionist. 'I'll see what I can do.'

The Neptunes were stopped for a moment by a pair of socks who tried to wrap round their eyes like blind-folds, but soon their war cries could be heard again charging even closer.

The receptionist rang her very hot boyfriend to see what he could do. 'He's a meteor,' explained the frilly sock. 'And although he is supposed to go to the sun to refuel, he said he'll drop you off at Earth on the way.'

'Yeh,' yahooed Zeke and Eppie as a blinding flash and a ball of light landed on the tarmac ready to take them home.

They ran as fast as fast across the tarmac with the Neptunes in frightening pursuit. Closer and closer, they could smell their fishy breath!

'Oh no, this is the end!' cried Zeke and Eppie as King Neptune lowered his enormous fork and prepared to

scoop the children up like two peas
on a plate.

'Ouch,' said Zeke.

'Ouch,' said Eppie when the prongs
of the fork poked and prodded them
as King Neptune tried to take perfect
aim.

'Aaaaaaaaaaaaagh,' they both
squeaked as they were scooped up at
last by the horrible Neptunes who
were laughing with glee until ...
suddenly a huge sock-trap dropped
from high above the tarmac and
captured the Neptunes like fish in a
net, leaving only the fork poking
outside and its passengers, Zeke and
Eppie.

'Phew,' said Zeke and Eppie as they
climbed on board the meteor just in
time, and waved thank you to the
clever socks. Then they swooped and
glided through the night.

It was very relaxing and the
children were feeling good until they

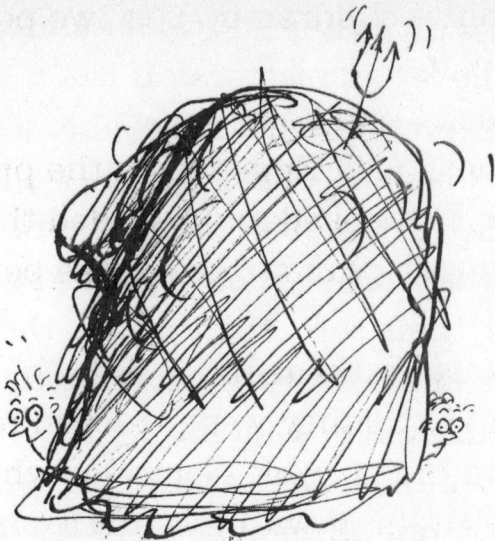

noticed, after a while, that the morning sun was teasing on the horizon and it was about to rise and wake the world.

'Mum will be getting up pretty soon,' whispered Eppie. 'I hope we're back in time!'

'I know,' said Zeke, 'I'm worried too. It feels like we're going far too s l o w l y wa

AA
AAA
AAH.'

Suddenly faster and faster they went, faster and faster and faster as they entered Earth's atmosphere!

The pressure of the speed stretched and pulled them: their faces, their arms, their legs, their bodies, their ears, their noses, their fingers and toes. Stretch, stretch, pull, pull—on it went all the way back to Earth. Until Zeke and Eppie were finally dropped off at their front door, both as thin as a piece of skinny spaghetti and as tall as a telegraph pole.

'Oh look at you,' Eppie laughed, as the light of the sun began to shine and they could finally see each other clearly.

'Well look at you,' said Zeke poking his long tongue out. 'And anyway, at least my yoyo's still safe on your head and that's really all that matters.'

'Is not all that matters.'

'Is so.'

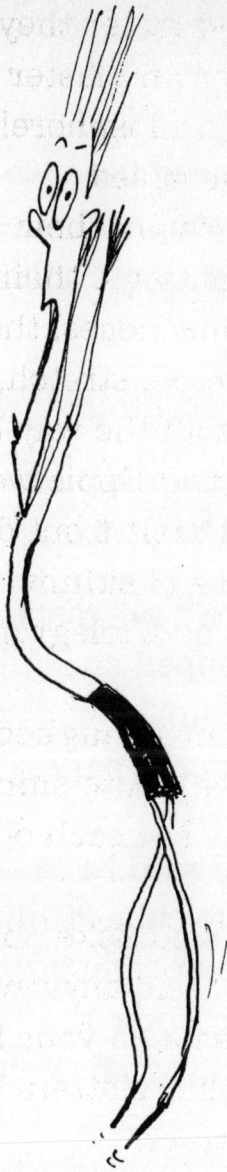

'Is not.'

'Is so.'

'Is not.'

And then they paused because they were both out of breath. And when they stopped fighting they could hear ... nothing.

Absolutely nothing.

Complete and utter silence.
(shhhhh)

'Oh no!' Zeke and Eppie gasped together. 'Mum's stopped snoring. She must be waking up.'
Aaaaaaaaagh panic panic panic panic.

'All we have to do,' said Zeke at last, when he'd finally calmed himself down, 'is get back to normal size and then Mum will never know the difference. So, first things first, let's go into our house.'

Which they did, by the easiest,

quietest way they could, which was
sliding underneath the front door.

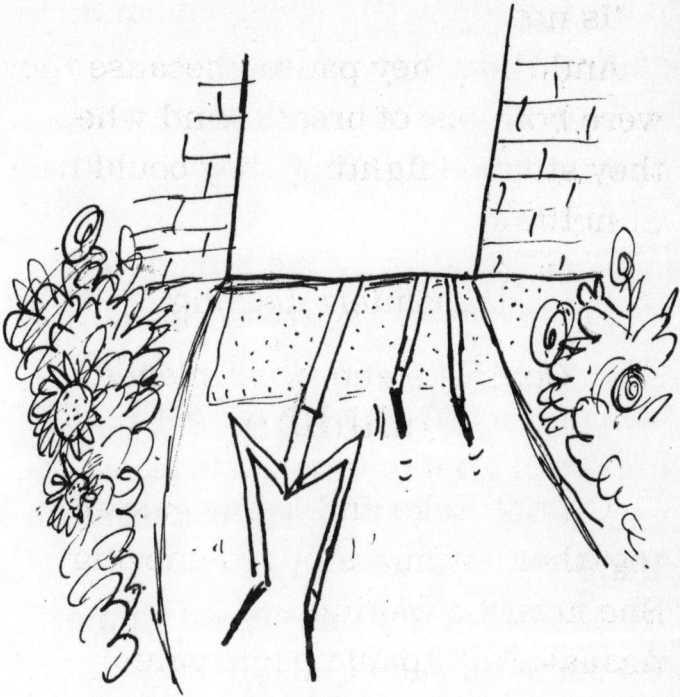

But when Zeke and Eppie stood up
they didn't fit under the ceiling, so
they crouched as low as possible,
bending over backwards, rolled into
balls, and full of fear they tip-toed up
the stairs. And they saw their mum
was still sort of asleep, only just

starting to stir and mumbling and
rumbling something about starting a
music group with her friends and
calling it the Spice Mums.

'Quick, into the bathroom!' said
Eppie to Zeke. 'And we'll work out
what to do.'

'Well I've already got a plan, you
stupid bossy boots,' said Zeke as they
closed the bathroom door. 'I think if
we run on the spot till we get really
hot, we'll go like warm soft plasticine
and we can mould ourselves back into
shape.'

'Good idea, for once,' said Eppie.
'So come on, let's get started.'

'No, first', said Zeke. 'Just to make
sure this trouble never happens
again, I think we should remove the
yoyo from your hair. So let's put
shampoo all over your head, to make
the hair slippery so the yoyo will
slide off ... absolutely easy peezy.'

'Good idea number two,' said Eppie

throwing her arms into the air with excitement and knocking Mum's perfumes off the cabinet so the bottles went smashing to the ground.

Snort, came the noise from Mum's bedroom. Oh no, she was waking up!

'Quick put the plug in the bath and stick your hair exactly under the tap,' said Zeke as he poured shampoo all over Eppie's head.

They could hear Mum's doorway opening wide and any minute they'd hear her footsteps coming down the hall.

'Rub your hair Eppie, to make it all slippery.'

But still the yoyo wouldn't come out. So desperately, Zeke added more shampoo and more and more and more, and before you know it the bath started to fill, and then began to overflow.

'I've got it!' said Zeke as

the room filled with bubbles. 'I've removed the yoyo from your hair. So turn the tap off and let the plug out immediately.'

But Eppie couldn't see where the plug was because of all the bubbles and the bathroom started to fill with water and enormous fabulous froth.

'What on *earth* is that coming under the bathroom door?' said Mum as she came stumbling down the hallway.

'Mum's coming!' yelled Zeke.

'Mum's coming!' yelled Eppie.

And they splashed around among
the bubbles, grabbing at this and that
and finally Eppie found the plug,
pulled at it hard and the water went
racing with enormous force,
tumbling thankfully down the drain.
But unfortunately so did long, skinny
Eppie.

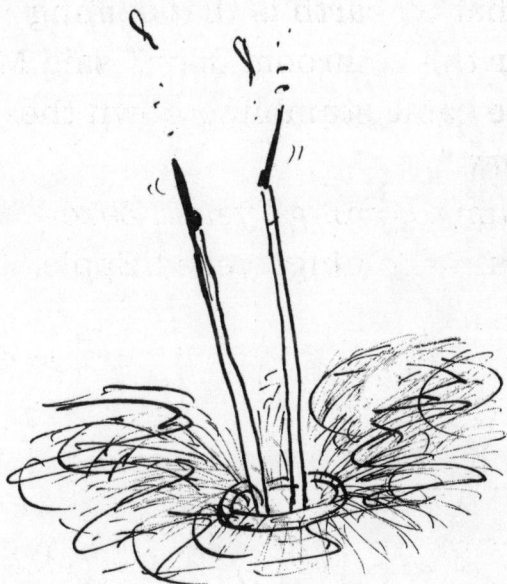

'Who's in there?' said Mum as she
knocked on the bathroom door.
'Whoever you are, you're in the most

humungous trouble and I'm coming
in to get you.'

And, with that, spaghetti Zeke
dived down the plughole after Eppie.

And Mum, who still hadn't found her glasses, walked straight into the laundry cupboard and got really angry with a broom.

My Sister's a Yoyo

When Eppie falls into a pot hole and gets
squashed to the size of a strawberry, her
brother Zeke decides to have some fun with
his yoyo.

What follows is a hilarious high tale of
escape, theft, bullies, brats, dobbers, goody-
goodies, garbage trucks, magic lamps, scabs,
snot, bribery, bravery, a blind mum, a fat
nurse, a skinny teacher and a boy on a
bicycle covered in vomit — and that's only
the beginning!

My Life is a Toilet

This is the tale of 15-year-old Fleur Trotter. It starts with a bad haircut and the sort of unattractive boy who makes mould look exciting and ends with the usual love, death, flood, fire, fortune telling and bust development.

'Without doubt the most honest and hilarious account of adolescent agony since The Bible*'*
— Fleur Trotter

'Lies' — Fleur's mother

'If Fleur gets this published she'll be up for adoption' — Fleur's father

'Fleur sucks. Who cares what *she does!'*
Miss Priss and Bum Face (Fleur's sisters)